ed vere

grumpy

PUFFIN

Hey!

I am <u>not</u> grumpy.

I'm hopping. See...

NOT grumpy!

And I'm green.

Green **ROCKS** my world!

Leaves are green...
YEAH!

Grass is green...
FISTPUMP!

DUDE! Frogs are green!

See...

NOT grumpy!

OK, OK. You're a HAPPY frog!

But you want to know what <u>doesn't</u> make me happy? I'll tell you...

OTHER COLOURS!

Red makes me cross.

Orange makes me dizzy!

Blue makes me <u>cry</u>.

Yellow schmellow.

Brown? Boooring.

Purple? WHY?!

But the worst...

PINK!

I do not <u>not</u> like pink.

Not one bit.

Uh-oh! Grumpy Frog alert!

Hey! I'm <u>NOT</u> grumpy!

Look...
I'm hopping with my friends.

All green, all hopping, all <u>happy</u>!
And I'm first!

I like winning.

But if I don't win...

<u>This</u> happens.

THAT is one grumpy frog.

Then my friends go off
and do **other** things.

I don't want to do other things.

Come and SWIM!

It's BLUE... No thank you!

I will not join in.

PAINT (GREEN)

who needs friends anyway?
I am perfectly happy on my log.

I'll just sit here,
alone,
and think...

WHY ISN'T EVERYTHING GREEN?

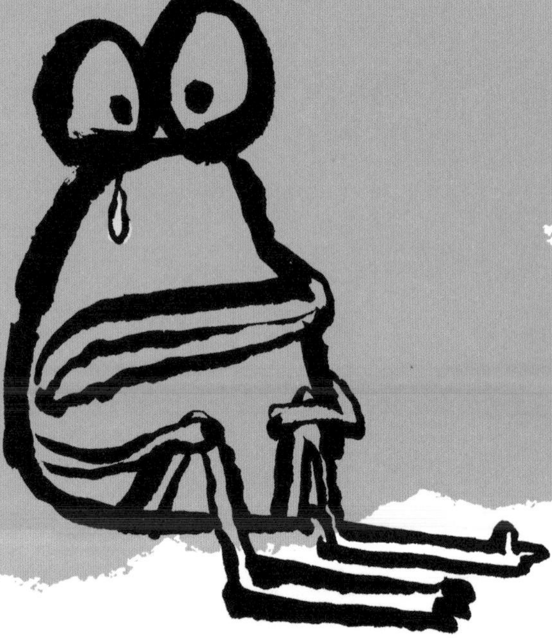

WHY do I eat flies?

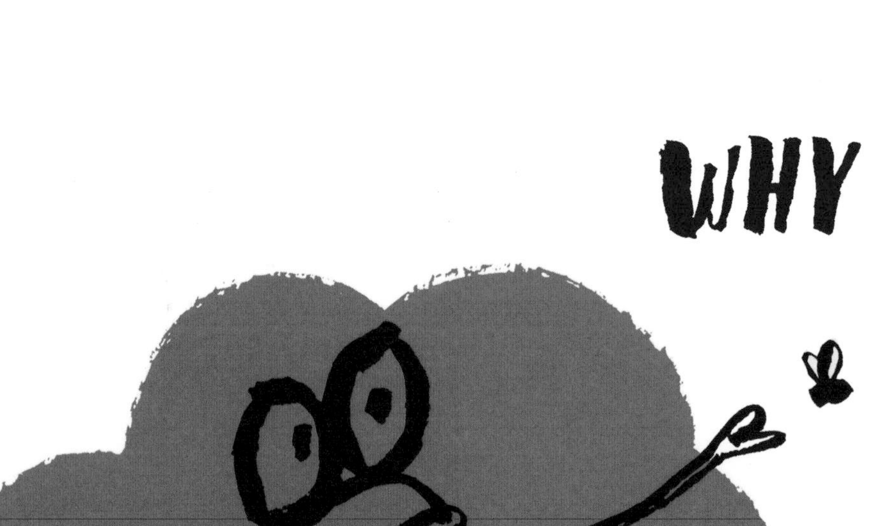

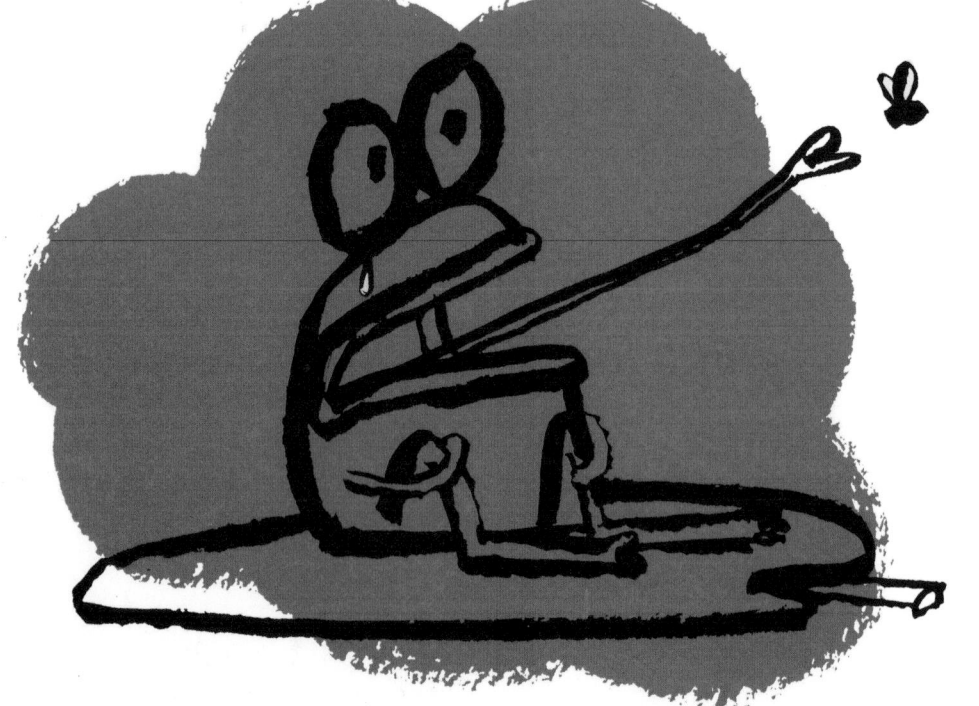

WHY isn't it my birthday TODAY?

WHY won't anyone hop with me?

I miss hopping.

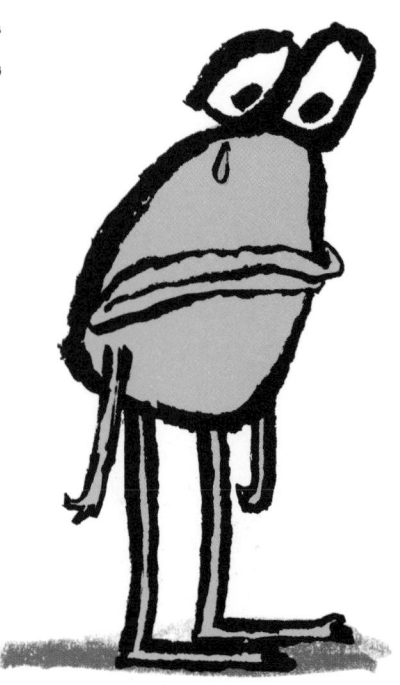

I miss my friends.

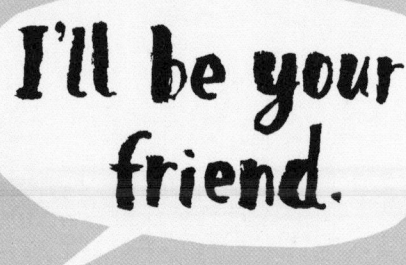

You are pink...

PINK!

I want my friends to be

GREEN!

"

Frog, that is grumpy <u>and</u> MEAN!

You are green!
Do you LOVE hopping too?

eating GRUMPY frogs.

SNAP!

Hey!

I am <u>not</u> grumpy.

oo

Am I?

Oh dear.

Was I grumpy with my friends?

Was I mean to Pink Rabbit?

Was I ?

I <u>was</u>!

I need to say sorry.

Excuse me, Crocodile...

Would you please let me out?

Since you ask so nicely... Of course!

I am a surprisingly reasonable crocodile.

And I only eat GRUMPY frogs.

Thank you very much.

I am sorry.

I was grumpy and I was mean.
Will you please forgive me?

Hooray! Let's all go for a lovely swim.

At last, the end of grumpiness.

DUDE! We all LOVE

hopping... together!

(And <u>I'm</u> first!)

Goodbye, Grumpy Frog.

Oi... <u>NOT</u> grumpy!

This is my resting face.

For my brother, Aidan (who is <u>never</u> grumpy)

With thanks to Andrea MacDonald and Goldy Broad

PUFFIN BOOKS
UK | USA | Canada | Ireland | Australia | India | New Zealand | South Africa
Puffin Books is part of the Penguin Random House group of companies
whose addresses can be found at global.penguinrandomhouse.com.
www.penguin.co.uk   www.puffin.co.uk   www.ladybird.co.uk

 Penguin
Random House
UK

First published 2017   001
Text and illustrations copyright © Ed Vere, 2017
The moral right of the author/illustrator has been asserted
Printed in China
A CIP catalogue record for this book is available from the British Library
Hardback ISBN: 978–0–141–37010–1   Paperback ISBN: 978–0–141–37011–8
All correspondence to: Puffin Books, Penguin Random House Children's
80 Strand, London WC2R 0RL

www.edvere.com   @ed_vere

FSC
www.fsc.org

MIX
Paper from
responsible sources
FSC® C018179